The Palmist and Other Stories

OrangeBooks Publication

1st Floor, Rajhans Arcade, Mall Road, Kohka, Bhilai, Chhattisgarh 490020
Website: **www.orangebooks.in**

First Edition, 2025

ISBN: 978-93-6554-825-9

Price: Rs. 299.00

Printed in India

THE PALMIST And OTHER Stories

AASIF SHAH

Orange Books Publication
www.orangebooks.in

"This book is dedicated to my lovely wife Mahamuda, and our adorable children, Daniyal and Yusra."

Contents

New Year's Resolution

‘‘You know the exact place?" I asked my friend who was walking with me. "Sure, it's somewhere here," he assured me. We were there to have his photograph, passport size, taken. But it seemed he had forgotten the location of the studio. It was late in the morning when the sun prepared itself for its ascendancy zenith-wards. Unlike in summer, we didn't walk under any shade. We were glad the sun had come out because the air was chilly, like on any other January morning. Yes, it was January, the first weekend. We had just celebrated Christmas and the New Year. We were still in the mood. It wouldn't leave us. We had such fun. "There it is!" His exclamation almost startled me. He pulled my coat sleeve to direct me to where the studio stood. There it was, indeed – a small yellow signboard. Block letters in blue colour read: SONNY STUDIO. It was clamped between two large stores. On the left was a bicycle shop, and on the right, a clothing store. It's a small space calling itself a photo studio.

We climbed up two steps before we entered. Already, I felt claustrophobic as always, as I do whenever I am inside a small, congested place. There was a bench cemented to the wall for customers to sit on. An old lady and a kid were seated on it, probably waiting for someone who had gone inside through the rectangular door that was cut out of the plywood board screen that partitioned the room, to have his or her photograph taken. Or maybe they were waiting for their turn. Half of the plywood board was well adorned with photos of various sizes. Full of smiling faces beamed up the otherwise dull background. I knew none of them; it's not expected of me either, anyway. The photographs were not done with on the screen only. Others were also there under a square glass plate on the desk behind which sat the manager. He was a Punjabi. "I want my passport - sized photograph to be taken," said my friend to him. "Colour or black and white?" he asked. "Colour." "It would be Rs. 20," he said as he made the receipt. "Please have a seat."

We sat down on the bench. My first guess of the old woman and the kid turned out to be true - a woman in her 30s came out from the other side of the screen through the rectangular hole. Of her being the mother of the kid, there was not the slightest doubt, because as soon as she came out, the kid clung to her. And the older woman was her mother - the similar faces could not have been explained otherwise. They left together. Next was my friend's turn. He went in. After a few minutes, he came out smiling.

"It's done," he said.

As we were making our exit, I asked the manager if we could come back in the evening rather than the "next morning" as was written on the receipt.

"No, yaar. Power shortages make our business miserable these days," he grieved, scratching his humongous beard. I took pity on him because he was right. We were on the road again. More and more people and vehicles filled up the road. The day's business had begun.

"So, have you decided on your New Year's resolutions?" said my friend.

"Not yet. I was still thinking this morning with my diary open, what my resolutions should be this year."

"Neither have I," he said at length, "but what's the use if we can't follow them?" Before I could answer him, my eyes caught something else on the ground. It was a pale yellowish envelope. I stooped down and picked it up. It turned out to be a photo envelope from the same studio which we had just left. It had the "SONNY STUDIO" trademark on it. Inside it was a roll of film which had been recently developed. Our curiosity got the better of us. Stepping aside lest we were knocked down by the incoming vehicles, we checked the negatives, holding them against the sun.

"Probably someone's Christmas party snaps," I said, looking at the negatives.

"No doubt," my friend replied. "Check out if there is a name and address on the envelope." Usually, on such envelopes, the addresses written are the name of the place in which the person resides, nothing else. The name was there - N. A. Najokpa, and the address was Langol, just the name of the place! Langol is a big area, and there are too many Najokpas - no way we could trace the owner of the envelope.

"What say?" asked my friend. "How about giving this back to the studio?" I suggested. "It's the best we can do." He agreed. As we turned to return to the studio, two youths on a scooter on the other side of the road stared at us as they passed us by. I stopped my movement for a few seconds. And then I stopped my friend's too and, instinctively, waved the envelope in my hand to them. They stopped immediately. The smiles on their faces could have beaten Julia Roberts on any given day. They parked their scooter, and one of them came up to us. "Najokpa?" I asked him. "That's my friend over there," he said, nodding his head at his friend. "Oh, we just found this on the road and we were thinking of giving it back to the studio where, coincidentally, my friend here also has just had his photograph taken." "That's very considerate of you, uncle," the young man was visibly jovial, "we were also going to the studio - it's a long shot but we decided to give it a try, just in case - and here we are!" "You are welcome, young man, but please don't give us the uncle tag - we are too young at heart, ha-ha!" roared my friend. After they had left, we continued our walk.

"I know what I am going to do this year," I said after a while.

"And what's that?"

"Improve my civility," I replied.

Ningol Chakkouba

"You can stop there, near the gate," Ibempishak said to the rickshaw puller. The rickshaw-puller stopped near a bamboo gate. The woman dismounted. Followed by her two little daughters, one after another. The *leirak* was almost deserted save for a few vehicles now and then. It bent abruptly after going on for some hundred metres. A tall and well-branched Gulmuhur tree stood to the left side.

"Here, take this," she said, handing him a battered five - rupee note. She picked up one of her children while the other clung to the tail of her *chadar*, and went inside the gate. The two girls looked neat and clean, but their clothes couldn't hide the fact that they were not new, even though they had been starched the previous day. Like any other child, they looked cute with their innocent eyes brightly open. The one in her mother's arms was four years old while the other was six years old. Their mother was on her *mapan naiba phanek* - a new one, which she recently had acquired thanks to a *marup*. Though it could not shield the paleness on her face. It was *ningol chakouba* day, one of the most important festivals of Manipur. It is perhaps a festival solely for the *ningol*-married women.

Ningol chakouba - the name itself reveals a lot, which is beyond explanation. The love between parents and daughters, between brothers and sisters, of exchange of blessings and gifts, all get reflected in a culture of benevolence. Ibempishak, a married ningol, arrived at her parental abode with her children as expected. As they entered, a *tulsi* plant in the middle of the courtyard could be seen. Behind it, some paces away, stood an old house. She called out for her mother, "*Ima*, *Ima*." An older lady came out from inside the house. "So you have come," said the mother with a glimmer in her eyes, as when mothers do when they know their daughter is coming after a long time. "Our babies look so beautiful today," she continued, taking the child from her daughter's arm. Just then, Boinao had also come in. When he saw his sister, he exclaimed, "*Eche*!" The respected word made

Ibempishak turn her head. As she saw where it came from, she too became jubilant. The two were the closest of all. "Thoibi has grown up!" he said, playfully lifting the younger of the two little girls. "Oh, Bem, you too!" he added as if not wanting to see the pout on the other child's lips. Both the children smiled.

"Who wants a chocolate?" "*Ei!*" chorused the girls. "Let's go, then!" "*Hoi! Hoi*!" Their uncle led them out. "He doesn't come as usual?" It was more of a question than a statement. It was asked by the grandmother.

"*Ahoi*, *Ima*!" the daughter replied with a bit of sorrow in her voice. "Would I be wrong if I said you are a fool? You always have been." "*Ima*, don't start again, please." "You didn't listen to us. You did what you liked - and see-where you are now." "Would you please stop, *Ima*, I didn't come here to hear that. It's for the sake of today that I come here - you know that." Nobody had forgiven her, except perhaps her sweet brother, Boinao. None had sympathised with her tears. She had become but an outsider - *jhat -houng- khrabi* ! Her *leikai* had disowned her openly. She had lost many of her friends, and the last blow was when the door was closed to her in her own house. All because she married a man of a different religion. As fate would have it, the husband turned out to be a broke and an alcoholic. Yet it was love that made her inseparable from him. "Naivety at its summit," her father repeatedly had said before he died, to anyone who cared to listen. At this point in time, a horn was heard.

"Eh! Your sister has come. Go inside. Stay in the back room. Fast! - and don't come out until they're gone," the old woman hushed her daughter in before she went out to receive the other.

Tharolei, the elder daughter, came in with her husband, a respected doctor. Unlike her younger sister, who eloped, she had a grand wedding ceremony. She had received every conceivable *potyeng* from her relatives, friends, invitees, etc. *Eche Leima* of Pishum had given her a washing machine; *Ine Chaobi* of Moirang had given her a stand fan; and so on. It was a grand wedding indeed. No, Ibempishak didn't attend the ceremony. At that time, the wound she had incurred was vivid. And anything about her would have added more disgrace to the family; today she remembered those relayed words of her late father. Moreover, the other party, the would-behusband's side, had strongly insisted that the words be kept under wraps for the time being. Ibempishak had endured all of it without a single pout. She had no right, had she? It would have been otherwise had she been married to a well-to-do person. Not so much fuss would have been there, then. Money sometimes talked; she learnt late in her life.

As Tharolei climbed up the two steps onto the varenda, she asked, "Hasn't she come?" "Not yet," her mother lied. Thaballei, the old mother, had two daughters. Both of them had come on this auspicious day to take her blessings. And she could not give them at the same time! Though she regretted her younger daughter's decision, she was still her own. She still loved her. She was the one whom she loved more. Everyone knew, too. An open secret in the family. And it was also she who received all her frustration without so much as a sigh. They knew each other well. "Ranjen, bring all the stuff in," Tharolei called out to her driver. While the husband and the mother-in-law, having exchanged formalities, had begun chatting. "*Ima*, where is Boinao?" Tharolei wanted to know. "Ah! That species! Not yet home, I suppose," her mother was least interested. "*O, Ima*," Tharolei said suddenly. "You know, it came positive this time. I am so happy." She was excited. "Oh, tell me it is true," the mother said, more excited. "Yes, mother," quipped the husband. "It's all his blessings." The news was great indeed. The only thing that was missing in the house of Gurumayum was the cries of a baby. It had been five years since they had been married. The happiness was visible.

"*Nungaiba paonidana, laklo laklo, chaba hourasi*," the mother led them inside the house for the grand feast that had been prepared since the wee hours of the morning.

*****

Ibempishak must have slept. It took two more shakes by her mother to wake her up. In that dusty room, the mother and daughter stared at each other for a few moments before the older opened her mouth, "Come, your food is getting cold." "Have they gone?" The question was there already.

"Yes, they have."

They came into a room where a feast must have been held, some time ago; the signs were still there. The daughter sat upon the *kouna* mat that was laid for her. And the mother served.

"Where is Boinao? - and where are their children?" It was the mother inside her that made Ibempishak ask the question. It was sudden, as if she had remembered - and with a pinch of anxiety.

"They went with Boinao. Don't worry, have your meal-you must be hungry," the grandmother calmed the mother down. Before she started with her plate, she took out a meticulously folded hundred - rupee note. Unfolded it carefully and placed it in front of her and cried, "*Ima, se, Boinao da pibiyu.*" "Hey! Don't you cry. Why must you cry?" She took up the currency note and told her daughter to carry on lest the food should be cold. "Yours is a *kourphu* and a steel *roughon* this year." it was so sudden and so interesting a subject that Ibempishak looked up. Thaballei smiled.

"Yes, it is," she continued as she brought out the two glistening items. They were her gifts. Out of curiosity, she asked, "What about sister--what did she get?" Her mother was about to answer, but the entrance of Boinao made her forget about it. Instead, she turned to him, "Where were you? Don't you know what it is that's today--and where are the children?"

Before Boinao could reply, a neighbour boy had come in running. "*Ine*", it was directed to Thaballei.

"*Ine* Hoinu told me to tell you to come fast. It's about them children." The mention of the children was more than enough for them to leave everything behind and run towards Hoinu's place.

As they reached the courtyard of Hoinu's house, a small crowd could be seen. On the veranda, upon a cot, Ibempishak's eldest daughter lay drenched. While the other was in the bosom of Hoinu, who was sitting on the edge of the cot, attending to the drowned child. The child looked lost; she breathed with sounds as if she were crying. And "*Ima*! *Ima*!" did not leave her lips. Boinao rushed to the child and tried to press her heart. A spurt of water came out of the child’s mouth. Everyone around wanted to help but did not know what to do. They all spoke at the same time.

“Don’t worry, nothing will happen. She is still breathing.”

“Doctor da pubana faroidra?”

“She is alive, just a few seconds inside water. Sanjoy had jumped in and brought her up immediately.”

All Ibempishak did was wail, "O, I am finished! I am finished!" and fainted near the foot of the cot.

The Wrong Beat

It could have been a sunny day had it not been for the incessant rain pouring down. It was that time of year when you know the thing coming is summer, but you're not quite sure whether the spring is over yet; when you know it rains sometimes during such a period, yet not the way it had been coming down so ceaselessly for several days.

There were six of us. *Ine*, her son and daughter, Anish and Chal Chal; *Imaton*; Amu, my friend and Anish's too; and myself. Having had our lunch, we were chatting on the veranda over black tea.

'What has our world come to? I've never seen such a downpour and that too at this time of the year,' *Ine* blew a complaint in the air as she put her tea down. Everybody agreed in unison.

'I think it's going to flood this time,' *Imaton* said.

'I think so too. Why, the river has risen high enough. It's a matter of two or three days before the flood if it continues at this rate.' Saying so, Anish took a loud sip of his tea.

'Stop that, it's irritating,' Chal Chal shrieked at him and was quick to add, 'and it's so boring to go to college too.'

'Hey, I didn't know we were having a weather conference,' Amu exclaimed in his typical funny way. Everybody laughed. I finished my tea and set the cup down on the side table.

'All right, Amu, tell us some stories to kill time,' cried *Ine*, as if suddenly realising his presence. She shook her teacup as if waiting for a prophecy.

'Oh! I don't have any news.'

'What about your daily duty?' *Imaton* shot at him with a teasing smile, sipping her tea.

'Ah! Yes, now with this rain, you must be a bit worried,' Chal Chal added the required salt.

'Forget it, you two! It's just a rumour. Who would go down there?' Amu threw out a laugh as if he was forced to do it.

He used to go to K____, our neighbouring village. Some said it was to meet his sweetheart. Others said it was just to hang out. But he did go there every single day. So, people had begun to call it his 'daily duty'.

'We all know about it, don't hide,' *Imaton* tried again. Everyone giggled.

'What time is it?' Anish asked, turning to me.

'Hmm...12.30,' I replied after checking my watch.

'Eh! Time has stopped, too,' he threw a lazy hand in the air.

'Why, is there anything special today?' I asked.

'Nay...' It'd just slipped out of his tongue when *Imaton* grasped the opportunity for another bout of her mollifying game, 'Do I smell a date here, Anish?'

The women turned their badger at him. Poor Anish! But he was saved that day. As I turned my head, I saw a man on a bicycle entering the gate. His left hand held the handle of the cycle while his right one held an umbrella. Seeing us, he smiled. After propping up his cycle against the mango tree near the gate, he strolled towards us. The women stopped their attack on Anish. *Ine* received him at the door. He was a familiar person but not a family friend. He was that sort of person from your village that you know by the face but nothing else. So we were a bit surprised by his visit. As soon as he saw *him,* Amu got up abruptly and went inside. It was so sudden and done in such a manner that calling it stealthy would not have been an exaggeration. But someone did see him in the process. Who can elude *Imaton's* eyes?

'Is Sir at home?' the man asked.

'Yes. What brings you here so unexpectedly? Do come in,' *Ine* ushered him in. He folded his umbrella before he came in. He was being seated on the chair vacated by her.

'Didn't he go office today?' he continued, as he sat down.

'He's feeling unwell since yesterday, so we thought he might take a rest,' *Ine* replied.

'OH I see. I just came to discuss something with him - if it would not disturb him, of course.'

'No, no, it won't. I'll tell him right away.' Saying so, *Ine* went inside.

All sat in an awkward silence. *Imaton*, the ever talkative, broke the ice, 'Tada, we heard you're a teacher at some high school.'

'You heard it right, Ichal, at N______ high school,' said the man.

'And the children? Oh, I almost forgot, go fetch tea for him, Chal Chal.' I don't know what had gotten inside her brain that she asked as such. Nevertheless, it was asked, and the man answered. Chal Chal went inside after collecting the empty cups.

'I've three. The eldest is a daughter who is doing her graduation in Lucknow. The second one is in SYJC while the third is in 8th standard.' If the man had shown a little confusion at first, there was no sign of it when he talked about his children.

'How is *Ine*?' *Imaton* didn't stop.

'She is fine.' Now he must be feeling uncomfortable sitting in front of her. And it must be a great relief for him that at that instance uncle came out. If not, God knows what would have been the next. Outside, the rain seemed heavier. Uncle was in his pyjamas. He looked tired with his unkempt hair and unshaven face. He was reluctant when he took the chair left by Chal Chal. He edged near the man. They exchanged a nod of acknowledgement.

'What can I do for you, pal?' Uncle leaned forward earnestly. Chal Chal came out with two cups of tea. Uncle and the man took one each from her.

'It's about a trifle thing. You know, I have a daughter who is in Lucknow doing her graduation,' the man took a pause and sipped his tea, 'Earlier I used to send her money by bank draft, but this time she said that the money be sent by money order. So, I thought it would be best to come to you. I already brought the money so as not to bother myself by going to the post office.' He withdrew some five hundred currency notes from his pocket.

When he finished counting them, uncle flashed a faint smile and said sympathetically, 'I could see you're mistaken. I am not what you're thinking I am. You should be in the adjacent house, the right one, not here. It's him, my brother, who works in the post office, not me.'

The man offered a sincere apology and smiled, and after downing the remaining tea, he excused himself. He proceeded towards the next house. Uncle smiled at us and said,' The world is full of funny people!' Saying so, he went inside with his cup of tea in his hands. Amu craned his head out of the door, and seeing that the man had left, he stepped out. He resumed his seat. *Imaton* did not delay as she caught him, 'Am I wrong to say I saw a fidgeting Amu when someone came in? Pray, tell us the meaning.'

All of us turned to Amu with a renewed curiosity, though we were also a bit confused.

'I almost went into a fit,' blurted out Amu with an excitement we usually experience when we think something's going to happen and it did not, 'I thought he found out all about us and was coming after me.'

'What are you talking about?' *Ine* asked the question that was on everyone's lips.

'Arre, he is the father of his "daily duty",' Anish explained it for everybody.

Aasif Shah

Ibohal

IBOHAL

It was in the month of December. The night was cold. The whole village was quiet. Elders were done with their evening prayer. And the womenfolk were busy in the kitchen, preparing dinner.

This year, the harvest was good. Ibohal was satisfied with what his paddy fields had produced. The small kitchen garden in their backyard had also been flourishing. His small pension would cover the other miscellaneous things. He was sure the coming year would be fine. He would not die of hunger, at least.

Ibohal was sixty - five years old. He was a pious and charitable man. Though he was not a rich man, he tried to help anyone who came to him for help. He was a highly respected old man in his village. His advice was often sought by young people and old alike. When asked to represent the village in the panchyat election, he turned down, saying others were more qualified than he.

Ibohal had two sons. Thoiba, the elder, was at I_______ for his higher studies. He went there after completing his matriculation in the village high school. He would come home during the holidays. And that would last a few days. The villagers didn't see him very often. Ibohal sometimes went to the city to meet him. His son would tell him everything was fine, and he didn't have to come. The son would remind the father that he could take care of himself now. Ibohal would come back satisfied.

Thoithoi, the younger one, was mentally retarded. The mysterious cause for it, as the story goes, was that when Thoithoi was ten years of age, he had killed a snake with a *loang* in their paddy field. Since then, he couldn't speak, and he began to live in his own world.

'The snake was a *lairembi,* a deity, and its spirit has possessed him,' so says a mother.

There was a belief in the village that the snake he had killed was the goddess of the field. And the elders said that her spirit had taken possession of his body. Ibohal believed. At first, he had tried *maiba maibis,* local healers, from far and near, but they couldn't cure his son. And then he took him to the doctors. They were also of no help. They prescribed medicines, but Thoithoi would not take them. Gradually, Ibohal had to take it as his fate.

The following year, his fields produced in abundance. Everybody talked about it. One of the *maibas* said it was because of the spirit that's inside Thoithoi. She was a good one, and so were the blessings. Ibohal readily believed him. He began to take extra care of his younger son. His friends also did the same. No children hounded his son anymore. Because their mothers warned them not to.

Having said his prayer, Ibohal entered into the kitchen where his younger son was sitting on a mat by the hearth. His wife was washing the utensils.

'*Ibungo*, do you feel cold?' he asked his son as he wrapped a shawl around his shoulders. The son nodded his head as if thanking him.

'What have you got for us tonight?' he asked his wife.

'*Hung-gaam*, of course,' she replied. *Hung-gaam*, mustard leaf, is a favourite dish during winter.

Suddenly, there was a blackout. If not for the fire from the hearth, there would have been total darkness in the small house.

'Wasn't it "load shedding" yesterday, and what could it be today?' Ibohal asked out loud. Dogs were barking outside. As he lit up the lantern, there was a knock on the door. At first, he hesitated. When it became louder, he got up and opened it.

'Who's there...?' he saw two young men in black leather jackets and faded blue jeans standing outside his door. One of them carried a big cricket bag on his shoulder. They were in their 20's.

'What's it, young men?' Ibohal asked.

'May we come in?' the one with the bag said softly.

'Strangers you are, but sure, do come in.'

The strangers looked about the room briskly.

'Sir, we are from I_______. We are salesmen. Unfortunately, today, we missed our bus. So would you be kind enough to let us stay here for tonight? We'll leave first thing in the morning tomorrow.' They had an amicable nature about them.

Ibohal had met a few salesmen who had come to his village before. These two men was none of them. Anyway, they were from I________ where his son was now staying.

'Please, be my guests.' Saying so, he turned towards the kitchen to his wife and told her to prepare dinner for them too.

'Thank you, sir, but don't trouble yourself with our meals,' the man without the bag said.

'But I insist. It is my principle that I provide food to those whom I consider to be my guests. Don't embarrass me. You must have food with us. And this is my eldest son's room where you will be sleeping.' Ibohal showed them his son's room.

'Where is he?' the first youth asked.

'He is in I_______, studying.'

They had dinner together. And after that, they chatted. They told the old man their names, *Leikais*, what goods they dealt in. They felt sorry that they didn't know the area where his son was staying. But they said they knew his college. They also promised to send a *maiba* from their locality for Thoithoi. He was a famous *maiba,* they assured him. They repeatedly thanked him for his generosity. Sometime later, they all slept.

The next morning, Ibohal woke up early. He went to his son's room to check on his guests. The door was open. He peeked inside - it was empty.

'Eh! These days' youngsters….' He never finished the sentence. It was the sound of the jeeps that stopped him. Three commandos came in, arms drawn as if ready to shoot. They dragged him out without saying anything. Other commandos scattered everywhere. They surrounded the house. The sun slowly rose. Inside one of the jeeps, two young men in black leather jackets and faded blue jeans lay as if they were logs. Blood smeared all over their bodies. Eyes were blindfolded. Their hands and feet were tied too.

A stern - looking commando, two - starred, came forward and asked Ibohal without caring to give any respect, 'Hey *ahund*, how long had they been here? How long had you known them?'

'Who, sir?' Ibohal was genuinely bewildered. Bhuch! A commando from behind knocked him down with his rifle butt.

'Get up.' The old man was pulled up by the collar.

'*Ahund,* tell us the truth, what were they doing here?'

When he got up, Ibohal caught a glimpse of the two bodies in the jeep. And then he understood everything. He replied truthfully, 'Sir, I didn't know. Never had I seen them before either. I just sheltered them.' His reply was met with a slap from the officer.

'Why did they choose your house?'

'How would I know, sir?' Bhuch! His knees! The old man screamed. The scream brought out his wife. When she saw them, she screamed too.

'What's this, sir?' she asked the interrogator, as she embraced her husband.

'You don't get involved. We have no woman constables here. So better stay out.'

'What do you mean? Just because you got a uniform does not mean that you can do whatever you want to.' Thambal spate fire. The commandos were taken by surprise. But Lairen, the officer, was nonchalant. He had seen too many of them.

'I am warning you again, lady, don't make me do what I don't want to do,' he warned. 'Hey, *hanuba*, don't waste our time. Tell us what you know about them fast.'

'I really don't know anything, sir.' Again, a butt landed on his back. He let out the pain loudly.

'Help! Help!' The wife screamed at the top of her lungs. It brought out some of the villagers from their houses. Many were woken up by it. By now, a small crowd had formed. But nobody came forward to say anything. They just watched quietly.

'Don't hit him again. He told you he didn't know anything. Hit me if you can, shameless.' Thambal went up to the officer, thumping her chest.

A commando pulled her aside by her hand.

'How dare you touch me, you shameless swine?' She glared at him, shrugging her hand off him.

'*Iche*, you are inviting trouble,' retorted the guy.

At the same time, the old man was receiving blow after blow. His screams were heard at the end of the village, as someone would boast days later.

Sensing that the interrogation was not going anywhere, the officer threatened the old man with every possible consequence in the book. The woman kept on wailing. She had become hysterical. Other women, who had by now come out, tried to console her. They also accused the commandos of attacking innocents and women; they called them names.

The villagers who were standing as spectators also became bold and started to speak up. At first, they murmured to each other and then turned to the commandos. One of the elders came forward and talked to the officer. The officer nodded vigorously.

'He is a very law - abiding old man, we know him well.'

'He won't do such a thing, never. There must be some mistake from your side, sir.'

He listened to them all. After some minutes, he told his boys to get into the vehicles. Just as they were doing so, there was a bang! Rat-tat-tat! It was the staccato sound of a carbine. Thoithoi was spraying bullets from a carbine.

The commandos were quick. They retaliated instantaneously. Thoithoi died on the spot. His bullet - ridden body lay in front of the door.

The officer received bullets in his thigh and shoulder. One of the commandos died on his way to the hospital. One minor who was standing among the crowd was injured in his neck. Fortunately, it was not critical, as it would be found out later on.

The morning was unusually sunny. The birds flew frighteningly up in the sky. The sound they produced and the sound that came out from the wailing on the ground vibrated throughout the whole village.

On March 20, 19---, Tikendra Thokchom, constable, was suspended for dereliction while on duty. It was from him that Thoithoi snatched the carbine.

Aasif Shah

Life's Like That

"I was shocked when I heard the news."

"It was too bad, incredible."

"It was only yesterday that they had a dinner party, no?"

"Forget about it, I saw him only this morning."

"I think I am still confused about his face."

"Arre, he had straight hair parted in the middle."

"Ok, I got it, he's a bit tall with a bright set of teeth, right?"

"Exactly."

"May their souls rest in peace."

"Amen."

"The other one was the one with big acne?"

"Yeah."

"They don't know how to swim?"

"No, none of them?"

"Then why on earth did they go there?"

"But then who would know it would happen like that?"

"At least they could have been more careful, na?"

"It was not like that - I mean - the place is their hanging out place. Not only for them but also for most of the kids in their place."

"But today there were none except them?"

"No, only four of them, as fate would have it. The story goes like this - they went there sometime after the afternoon. There an elevated ladder - like steps in the middle of the dam. These two guys climbed the steps. And one of them, the acne one, reached the top. The other took out his mobile to click snaps, but it slipped, and he lost control while trying to retrieve it. You know how it is at the foot of a dam. The guy was struggling with those depressions. All of them were screaming but none dared to dive. This guy on the top dived and he too drowned, to put it matter-of-factly."

"Shit."

"The other two who were on the bridge were screaming like anything, but nobody came to their rescue. They just watched their friends drown in frustration. The tears came down naturally. There is a village nearby. One of them ran there and begged everyone he met for help. But nobody was ready. He told them he would give them whatever they wanted. He handed them his wallet and mobile. But none came forward to go with him."

"Why didn't he call up the police?"

He did that. But you know these fools, they kept asking stupid questions, wasting precious time. At last, as he was about to leave, one of the elders told him the contact number of the fire brigade station. He also helped him contact them. But the irony is, those fighters told them they needed police authority as it involved dead persons."

"Shit."

"The elder man persuaded them, and after an hour, they heard the siren. It was the police. Together they came to the spot. The elder man was with them, too. There, they found the other guy totally numbed. He was scared to death. Who would not? He just saw his friends disappear, swallowed by the gloomy roaring water. He told them where they vanished. A fire-brigade vehicle also just arrived. And a rescue team suddenly came to life."

"Horrible man, see my goose bumps. Did they find them?"

"They found one, but they are still searching for the other, the acne one."

"God save us all."

"Shit, it's already 2 o'clock. Ok. Goodnight. Let's get some sleep."

I put off the light. I thought about the incident. I just could not come to terms with it.

I didn't know when I slept, but when I woke up the next morning, my roommate had already gone to college. It was already 9.30 AM.

I was bored with going to college, so I went down to the internet room. Our hostel has an internet room with 30 computers. Luckily, I got a free PC. Just as I was about to log in, the guy next to me asked me for a pen.

"I don't – hey - aren't you dead?" It was the only line that I could come up with when I saw him sitting next to me.

"You were mistaken, he was my roommate."

Aasif Shah

Missed Chance

It was a bad day. It was a bad day for him indeed. Not a bit of luck. Why it was so, he did not know. It was not the kind of day he would have chosen had he had the power. But he did not possess the power. So he took it as it was. A firm determination was taken - a determination to do something fast. Because the butterflies in his stomach wouldn't just stop fluttering. He had not had a morsel of anything since morning. Neither a 'pick'. It was late in the afternoon. Shyamlal was a thief by profession. An expert in pick-pocketing. Today, as he descended the slanting pavement onto the railway platform, he seemed quite unwilling. His face was expressionless. The face was square with two keen, inquisitive eyes and a sharply pointed nose. The hair was well - oiled and perfectly parted at the side. A man of twenty , in shirt and trousers: he didn't look like any of those shabby beggars or thugs who infest railway stations. By his appearance, he looked like any other gentleman waiting for a late train. The railway platform where he stood wore a deserted look except for a few passengers, cobblers, beggars and a lone policeman with his stick in his hand. He looked more like a chowkidar of an old dilapidated building. His presence did not affect Shyamlal's mind, which knew that all railway stations save one or two would be almost deserted at that time. It was the time when the public usually had lunch or did not want to go outside due to the intense sun, and surely not the time to go to offices, schools, colleges, etc or to return from them. Yet, he knew, trains would come full. That's why he still had the patience to wait for them. It was inside a compartment, a crowded one, where he would try his hand at this afternoon. An experienced pick-pocket, he seldom trusted his luck. He had long given up the idea of becoming somebody or hitting upon a jackpot someday. He had known the world, or rather had experienced it to some extent, to buy those sorts of childhood fantasies. The 'game' as he called it, started when he was still a child, when he was under the tutelage of his 'uncle' - an old man who was a master pick-pocket in his own right. The old man was not his real uncle. They were not blood relatives. It didn't make a difference that the old man was a bachelor. They had been living together since that day when the older man had found him, a baby, lying on the steps of the temple crying. No, his uncle was not there to pray but to find prey. The baby was given a name - Shyamlal. God knows why! Shyamlal learnt many tricks from him. Some were outdated. Some were still useful. He knew every trick in the book. He could tell where a man keeps his wallet, or money if there's no wallet, by a matter of a mere glance or a slight touch. His judgment was seldom wrong. Though he had been caught a few times and had been behind bars too, it didn't deter him from indulging in his livelihood. The mistakes were due to plain carelessness, he would boast among his peers. None argued.

Standing on the platform, he was feeling different. He could not remember a day he was not successful. 'Is this going to be the first one?' he thought as he scrutinised the people around him. His trained eyes didn't miss much. What he saw was not promising. There was a probable though - an old man in a kurta and dhoti - his money inside a knotted handkerchief inside his kurta pocket, left side. But he was reluctant. He let him go. He reminded him of his uncle. A flicker of a grin appeared on his face as he heard an announcement on the public speaker system. It warned to be careful of pick-pockets, to take care of one's belongings, to report any suspicious activity to the railway station master, blah, blah......it also announced the arrival of a train from Belahpur and which would be heading for the CST station. He looked up at the display board. The train was late by seven minutes. Nevertheless, it crawled in stealthily. Unlike inter-state ones that arrive loud and clear, local trains slither in silently like a snake trailing its prey, becoming a good reason for many a death on the tracks.

The train was full as he had anticipated. The crowd began to alight even before the train was halted. As if in synchrony, the station suddenly became full of people. A commotion developed within a second. Though he could easily reach out a hand and relieve a gullible fellow of his wallet, Shyamlal didn't. He would do it inside a compartment, he thought. A compartment was chosen for the execution to be carried out. It was full to its capacity. He saw him. He kept one of his legs inside while the other was still outside, connected with the platform. With his hand tightly clutching the pole inside, he waited for the train to move. It was his habit to do like that. Just as the train started, there was a sudden tumult. He could hear chor! chor! He turned his head. Then he let go of the train. The crook was running for his life, running towards his doom. He didn't see Shyamlal waiting for him a few yards away from the train, which had just left. And when he became aware of him, it was too late. The front kick landed exactly on his chest, and he fell flat on the ground. A knotted handkerchief was in his left palm. If it were not for the policeman, the lean crook would have been into pieces, what with the crowd surrounding him. The timely act of the man in uniform saved him from a god-knows-what kind of a thrashing. Shyamlal was praised for his bravery. Many took his hand into theirs. He was lifted in the air by the joyous crowd. It made him feel awkward. He doubted whether they were genuine.

However, he received them with a planted smile on his face. It was his duty, he repeatedly reminded them. His mind was somewhere else. The sight of the handkerchief could have instilled him, but he didn't know for sure why he had done it. The poor chap must be desperate, he thought. He had not seen him before, either. Maybe he was an amateur. Maybe he did the right thing - saved him - he reasoned.

As he waited for another train to arrive, he thought of the compartment which was full to its capacity. Among the crowd, a yawning fat man with a fat breast pocket: his missed chance.

Aliya

The train reached the station early in the morning. Outside the station, the sky stretched far over him. The buildings were four- to five-storey tall. They uniformly lined the street. Closed shops stood with sombre carelessness. ‘‘My home is inside that gully," his friend said. They had walked five minutes from the station. There was a gully ahead between two lines of apartment buildings.

His friend's house was a small bungalow. They were greeted by his friend's mother, who was wrapped in a cream shawl. She had kept tea ready for them. After spending a night on a train journey, the tea was a welcome treat. His friend took him to his room after the tea. He was not introduced to the woman. It was fine by him. He was shy of women, young and old. And it seemed the woman was used to it. It was only when he was lying in the bed next to his snoring friend, looking at the ceiling fan, that he remembered she was mute. His friend had forgotten to switch on the fan. He thought, two days and I would be off.

“We’ll go post lunch. I’ve a bike. It's just a few minutes ride," his friend had mumbled.

The sight punched him: rows of orange trees on either side of the road. They had reached their destination. The fragrance from the trees ran towards him in groups with open arms. He wondered in amazement. Tinted green leaves and shaded green-yellowish oranges, with a bunch of white blossoms in each tree, formed an impression on his mind. Excited and curious, he started clicking photos of them with his mobile phone. His friend explained the varieties and how they were grown. The harvesting time was nearing, he said. He took notes on his mobile. "These oranges have already been sold to the buyers. This tree here is ours, though," he said, tapping a particular tree. The blinding sun was obstinately piercing. Thankfully, he had a cap on. By evening, he had almost carved his footprints on the ground with his overenthusiastic walk. His friend had long resigned himself to the farm hut, made up of mud, erected at one corner of the farm. He entered the hut sweaty and dusty.

“You done?" his friend was lying on the only charpoy. He was smoking. Two things hung from the ceiling: a swing and a bulb. There was a hearth and some black bottom utensils at a corner. Sunlight forced in through a square opening in the wall. There was also a *matka* for water. ‘‘It’s so crazy, bro. Thanks for bringing me here," he clapped his friend's arm. His friend gave him water from the *matka* and said, "Let's go. My uncle might need the bike." He said he wanted to stay a little longer. "Call me when you are done. I’ll come pick you up." His friend left. He plucked the grass near his feet as he sat outside the hut and gazed at the trees. After a long time, his leisure was disturbed by a ruffling sound inside. When he got inside, he found a pigeon limping among the utensils. He took it up and had a look. Its left thigh was ruptured. He caressed it. It cooed. As he came out, he saw her standing a few steps away from the door. He stood like a Chinese terracotta soldier. She looked like a bright ripe orange that one wants to hold in one's hand forever. The girlish bubble perched on the edge of the woman of sublime perfection she was turning into. She was in a green salwar kameez, with a blue dupatta, that clung to her buxom as if it was trying to magnify her flawless maturity. Solemnity of the softening sun shone on her structure. Her childhood innocence is still etched in her beauty. Her face was like the reddish orange evening sky after a hard sun. Her auburn hair curled coyly on her shoulders. He looked at her. She looked at him. The equilibrium in his system was poised like the balancing of a rope walker.

"Pigeon she gestured with her chin. He realised the warmth of the feathers in his hands. She took the pigeon and went away. He felt wretched. He regretted everything. He ran out and looked at her walking across the farm till she became a bobbing dot and disappeared into the dusk. She did look back twice from two different points. He took a photo of himself. He looked like a 21-year-old fool. He deleted it. When he tried to phone his friend, he found out his mobile had no balance. Since his network was roaming, he couldn't receive calls either. It was night already. He could see the city shimmering at a distance. After trying thoughtfully chosen paths, he concluded that he was lost. He was hungry. Everything around him seemed to be growing taller and slimmer. He stood under a tree, tired.

A bullock cart came his way. The *cartwallah* was a moustachioed, thin, turbaned fellow. The bull, with a big bell around its neck, was thrice bigger than he. He asked him where the station was. He got an answer in Marathi. He couldn't understand. The *cartwallah* waved his hand as if to say Hop on. He did. The bell's clink mingled with the wheel's squeak as the cart pulled on through the night.

After a while, they stopped in front of a dimly lit old cottage. He was baffled. A smartly dressed man came out. The face looked familiar, but he couldn't place him.

"Hi, I am Nehru." Nehru clasped his hands as he helped him get off the cart. His hair was tersely parted at the side. "*Chacha* Nehru?"

Nehru shrugged it off as if it was the most normal thing to hear and said, "We need a strong foundation, for that we need education. We must educate our children; only then do we have a future for them. I am expecting Gandhi anytime now. Young man, you look pale. What is the matter?"

“I saw this girl at my friend's uncle's farm.” “Young man, be bold. Speak to her. Many a man missed the chance for the simple reason that they failed to initiate the talk. Time is always ripening to a moment; when it comes, you should gather it, or otherwise it would rot away. We have a clandestine meeting. Let’s get inside lest the British should suspect something." He said he had to go to his friend's place. Nehru patted him goodnight and went inside. The bullock cart materialised again. He hopped on it. He couldn't just understand it all. He closed his eyes. When he opened them, they were on the main road. The *cartwallah* dropped him near a junction and pointed him to a left turn and left. He kept walking, unsure. Finally, he found his friend's place. There was restlessness in the house. It was that his friend had gone to the farm to look for him twice. He didn't tell them where he had gone lest they should take him as mad. That night, he could not sleep. He rejected the idea of asking his friend. What would he think of me? She lingered in his thoughts as the tune of a catchy song one just heard. The next day, he saw her crossing the gully that was in front of his friend's house. He went up to her.

“How is the pigeon?"

“What are you doing? People are watching, please go away," she said. He was taken aback. ‘‘Wait for me at the road," she whispered. He walked ahead. "She's fine now, thank you. You are Ajmal's friend, right?" They're walking on the road. "I'm Suhail. We're roommates in a hostel. We came down here yesterday. I've a project on oranges as my project for the third year. What's that in your hand?"

“A Tale of Two Cities. Our classic. BA first year. Have you read this book?’’

“Yes, it’s interesting," he lied lest she should stop talking to him. ‘‘This is my precious book.’’

It was a hardcover book. They had reached her college. He noticed how different she looked. She was in a yellow floral printed kurti and blue jeans. ‘‘Can we meet again?" he asked. ‘‘Why?" "I’ll be at the farm in the evening." She strolled inside without answering.

“You know this is their tree. We can have orange from this one, “Suhail said as he plucked one, “you want one? “She told him they were unripe. He tasted it, and it was sour. He threw it away. They walked to the hut. She told him about her pigeons at home. He told her about the oranges. He showed her the pictures he had taken. She played with his phone. ‘‘I am also getting a mobile on my birthday," she said. ‘‘When’s your birthday?" ‘‘Next month." ‘‘Wait, please stay still." Suhail leaned towards her. She was startled. He picked up a single eyelash that was below her eye with his fingers as delicately as if he were picking up a stamen of a flower in his lab. Her eyeball flitted everywhere except at him. He put the eyelash on his palm and said: Wish. She blew it and broke into laughter. If laughter were flowers, her laughter would have glowed in the night. He observed tiny reddish hair on her jawline near her ear that perfectly blended with her skin. He was sad. He could not think of leaving her. He wanted to take her everywhere he went. It was strange. She said it was getting late.

"I'm leaving tomorrow evening."

She sucked up the sound of the hut and strode out. The void of silence gathered on her book and a pen which he saw on the charpoy. He opened it. *Aliya* was written on the first page. He wrote his number on the back of the last page. He came out. She had already gone ahead. He caught up with her and handed her the book and the pen. "Oh, thanks." On the way back, Suhail told her about the strange incident of the previous night. She refused to believe it, terming it as nonsense. "You walk ahead," she said as they were nearing the buildings. He walked up ahead. She waited till he was a little further and crossed the road. When everybody had slept, Suhail got up from his bed and tiptoed out of the house. He went to Aliya's house with a great fear of what if someone sees him. Her house was three houses away. A window was open with the lights on. He looked into it. Aliya was writing something. He threw a pebble at her. When she saw him, her eyes became as big as two moons.

"What are you doing here?" Aliya screeched as softly as she could. "I just wanted to see your pigeons. "Very funny." "Lucie is there," she pointed. The limping pigeon was at the farthest corner away from the rest. The pigeons sat like feathered conchs inside a plywood box especially made for them. The stench was harsh. "She has a name?" "Yes. The heroine in the book." They spoke in whispers. "Have you read the book today?" "No mood to read." The words came to Suhail as if they were hot irons.

A sound cracked somewhere. Aliya put a finger to her lips. She craned her neck to see if anybody had woken up. Her father had come out of the house. They crouched behind the box. Her father went to the other side, where the bathroom was. They didn't move. When her father went inside the house again, they stood up and let out the lumps in their throats. She led him to a bench behind the house. They sat down. The moon looked like a snowball. Each knew what each of them was thinking. They were afraid to bring the words forward. It might break one of them, or both. She watched the moon; he watched her and wished the moon had dropped in his hands. It's a moment like this that one should cultivate so that it can be picked out of one's memory when at leisure. Inside her room, Aliya propped on her pillows with her precious book. She turned over the first page. She continued till she reached the second last page. She smiled and closed the book. The next evening, they were at the station. Nagpur station was at its busiest and noisiest. Ajmal and Suhail kept their bags under their seats and sat down. Ajmal's mother and others were at the window. Suhail thanked her for her hospitality. She blessed him by running her palm on his head. The train was leaving in five minutes. Suhail's chest was jammed. Aliya had not come to the station. He kept looking expectantly, yet there was no sign of her. Then he saw her. She was hiding behind a bookstall. ''You want something? I'll just come," he said to Ajmal and ran off before Ajmal could answer.

He jumped off the door and ran towards the stall. She was in an orange t-shirt and white capri pants. They looked at each other without speaking. She gave him a wrapped gift. “I thought you'd like to have something on the way." “Thank you," he said as he took the gift. Too many things were running through his head. On her part, she was trying to look brave. “All the best with your project,” she said.

“I hope you read your precious book well,” he said and waited for her reaction. It didn't come. The sudden blare of the warning horn from the train cut their silence.

“Have a safe journey. Now go, they'd find you missing,” she lilted. The platform started moving as he looked out the window. He sat straight as he had tucked the gift on his back under his shirt. She became smaller and smaller on the platform as the train moved out. At last, the station was far behind with all its unsaid thoughts. Everyone was preparing to sleep. The train was cruising at full speed. Suhail bade Ajmal goodnight and climbed up on his upper berth. As the lights of the compartment were put off, he took out the gift and opened it. It was her copy of A Tale of Two Cities.

The Lunch

When he reached the restaurant, he saw a sign on the door. It said it was closed for the day. His stomach's hopes shattered. It was a hard day for him. He had neither picked a single pocket nor had he eaten anything since morning. The sun was as hot as it could be on a July day. He ran his fingers through his hair. His fingers felt sticky. The restaurant was the only place where he could have bought food on credit, if not for free. He cursed the manager. He looked around. A few pedestrians walked on the road. Fewer vehicles passed by.

As he climbed down the steps, a hand tapped on his shoulder.

'Hi, Rajesh, what a pleasant surprise!' A fashionably dressed young woman showed her sparkling teeth. A big designer bag slung over her small shoulder.

'Oh, hi,' he said, shaking hands with her.

'How have you been? It's been a long time. What's this with your stubble – oh, is it in again? It looks good on you, though.'

'What are you doing here?' he asked.

'Oh! I work here - next block - I came out to have lunch. Have you taken lunch? Come, I am hungry, there's a lot of catching up to do, we'll do it over lunch. Come, come, I know a place here which serves amazing prawns.'

He resisted when he saw the restaurant. She insisted. It was a posh restaurant, a league way beyond his budget. Yet, he followed her inside.

A smartly dressed waiter guided them to a table, always smiling. She kept her handbag on an empty chair between them. His eyes stayed a moment late on it.

'It's just a first copy. Nice, no?' she winked at him as she took her chair. 'So, how's Saina? Has she completed her design course? Of course, she must have. I like the way you look - shabby yet cute. I know she must be having a boutique and all. Is it going well? I am sure it is. She's just well cut out for the job. It's really easy for her. She knew all along what she wanted to do. Unlike us. We were just the normal types, I guess. 9-5 people. We still are.'

He nodded now and then as he concentrated on his prawns.

'I had a crush on you, you know.'

He raised his left eyebrow and smiled without showing his yellow teeth. 'That's sweet of you.'

'I was so young then, Saina used to tease me a lot. And how's everything with you? Oh god, have I been talking and talking?' she laughed, waving her fork in the air as if it were a magic wand.

‘Oh no, please, I like hearing you.’ He smiled.

‘So what’s up with you?’

'Well, I am into this....’

'Oh, I am late, I have to rush back. It was great bumping into you. Cheque, please.' She tilted her head to the smiling waiter.

When the bill came, he took it up as if he were lifting a bag of lead.

‘No, no! Some other time, please,' she snatched it from him.

They bade goodbye in front of the restaurant. She got into a cab and waved her hand from inside. He looked till the car took a turn and vanished from his sight.

He felt the new 500 rupee note in his coat pocket and muttered, 'God bless Rajesh, whoever he is.'

Trend Setters

'Isn't it beautiful?' said the mouse to the cockroach.

'It's a dishonest flag over there. it does not define freedom. we are not free.'

'It's a pity. beauty is a pity if we don't exist.'

'We'll set an example.'

They were on top of a castle, which lay alone on a small island, surrounded by a lake and mountains beyond it. they were madly in love. but the brother cockroach had found out about them and told Father Cockroach. it was their first crime. Inter-family tie was a black stain to their honour. father cockroach went to the mice colony that lived on the ground floor. One thing led to another, and a huge fight broke out between the two families. Both families swore they would kill the lovers if they met again.

Finally, the matter was brought to the council of big cats, the ruler of the castle. she called for an assembly. everyone came: the families of mice, cockroaches, dogs, cats, lizards and insects. The two lovers stood with their own families. After hearing from both sides, the big cat closed her eyes in deep thinking. She opened her eyes. Everyone looked at her in anticipation.

'Both the families should reconcile,' said she, 'the lovers are to be sent away for three months to separate mountains as punishment.' Everybody clapped. they were satisfied with the judgment. Except the lovers. Their hearts openly grieved. It was yesterday. Today, when everyone was taking an afternoon nap, they came up on the terrace of the castle, from separate routes, and met. This was their second crime. it's forbidden to climb to the top in the afternoon.

'Are you ready?' asked the cockroach.

Mother mouse noticed her daughter's absence first. she sounded an alarm. Father Mouse took some goons and went up the stairs. The cockroaches lived on the 3rd floor. There, they found the cockroaches were also planning to come to them to take back their son, who they thought had been kidnapped by the mouse family.

A wise old dog enlightened the situation and helped in organising a search unit. that's when the mother mouse came running.

'I am ready,' the mouse looked intently into the cockroach's glinting eyes. they kissed, closed their eyes and held each other's hands. Just as they were about to jump off the castle, a dog shouted their names. dogs, cats, mice, cockroaches, lizards, and insects came running behind him. They were panting. Mother mouse ran to her daughter and hugged her.

'We will marry you two. Please don't think of doing such drastic things ever. Please forgive us, I read your note,' she said between sobs.

'Why on earth would you leave a note?' The cockroach wanted to know.

'It was not a note. I wrote it to remind myself.'

They got married that evening. Inter-family marriages were declared lawful in the castle ever since. But climbing to the top in the afternoon was still a crime.

Aasif Shah

The Palmist

When I came out after enjoying a treat of breathtaking paintings, the sun was too much for me. So I sat on the steps of the gallery. Just as I sat down, I saw him. I was startled. I went to him and greeted him in our indigenous lingo. He looked amazed. Then he sprang up and hugged me.

'What are you doing here?' I asked.

'That's a long story. First, tell me how come you are here?' he countered.

We both smiled. I told him I had come to Mumbai to visit the various art galleries as a part of my project.

'Well, I am doing a great business here,' he boasted.

'And what is it?' I was curious.

'Palmistry,' he replied.

'You what?' I was shocked. I never knew he had done any palmistry thing in his life. Ha, what a joke! Forget about him, I do not know of anybody inside his clan who is considered one.

'My friend, I know as well as you do very clearly - you are not such a person, you never were.'

'I was not before. I am now.'

'Oh, I see!' I broadened my eyes without seeing anything.

'No, you don't,' he said. 'You know, my father started all this. He was here before me....'

'Eh! Your father, you say?'

'Let me finish. If you don’t believe me, look at that news-clip over there.'

Sure enough, there was an old newspaper clipping. It was hung on the fence. At close observation, it was in fact a genuine article on Subash Chatterjee, the palmist - my goodness!

"The future at Kala Ghoda"

The title read in bold black. I felt intrigued. Never had I heard Subash Chatterjee being a soothsayer or whatever. I know him. I used to play with his son, Shyam Chatterjee, who was now talking to me. A long time ago, he suddenly disappeared. My interest started to grow.

'What say?' he winked at me.

'You beat me!' I smiled back. 'How on earth is this possible?'

'Don't waste your energy on that,' he chuckled.

'Shyam, tell me your secrets, I am curious.'

'Of course, I will tell you,' he gave a pat on my shoulder.

'All you have to do is follow the person's mind you are engaging with,' he had begun giving out his secrets!

'I think I don't understand,' I said as we sat down.

He spat out paan-stained spittle. His mouth was as red as blood as he spoke.

'See,' he whispered, 'suppose, you have to tell the lines on a person's palm, how'd you do it? Tell that person, first of all, he has a few great lines - everybody has them, you know. After doing that, casually ask his date of birth. And when he tells you, recall what you have read about that zodiac from the morning newspapers, and tell him.'

'And get a nice slap if he happens to have read the same thing,' I replied.

'Never! You don't know these people,' he gestured with his hands to emphasise what he was saying. 'Even if they had read the same thing, they'd think I am not a fake because I tell them what they think is true because the papers also said the same thing this morning.' It was like a kick in my stomach.

'As simple as that?'

'No! You also have to read a lot of books and should act masterfully. It's all about acting, too,' he explained. 'And one of my best weapons is....' he couldn't finish the sentence. A young couple had stood in front of us. The girl seemed fascinated by the cards on which human palms with various lines were drawn. But her boyfriend was not finding them amusing.

'I want you to have a look at his lines, Baba,' said the girl.

'Of course, young lady,' my friend said in a willing tone.

'Well, Baba, he is a non-believer,' said the girl holding her man.

'Young man, never disrespect Kali Maa if I have to advise you,' Baba said with extreme seriousness. I listened intently. 'And let me tell you before you come near me,' he continued, 'there's a mole on your right hand.'

The young man, who until now had not been giving any heed, gave a startled look. Automatically, he took his hand out of his pocket.

'How'd you know that?' The words trembled out. I was dumbfounded.

'Never underestimate my power,' the guru now had captured his pupil. The pupil stretched out his hand. It was not taken in, though. Instead, the palmist told him to lay down Rs. 200 on the mat as his fees. The money appeared in a jiffy.

Shyam put on his specs, took out a simple magnifying glass from a wooden box and took the man's hand into his. He studied the lines carefully.

'Ah! You have a few great lines,' he said. I grinned. The young man got interested.

'Recently you got a job but, umm,' the palmist brought up the palm nearer to his magnifying glass. 'But someone took it from you, is that so?'

'Yes, baba,' the young couple was excited. I was bewildered.

'Don't worry, you have another coming. This time you will get it. The girl next to you is of good luck,' he spoke without looking up. The love-birds smiled.

'You have lost some money too. And you have bad relations with your neighbours nowadays.'

'See if there is any amount of money coming my way,' the man asked.

'Umm......yes. Some amount could be seen. Probably on Thursday you will get it.'

The two asked many questions regarding everything to which my friend answered to their satisfaction, as could be seen from their beaming faces. The young man had become a convert. The whole business took about forty-five minutes.

After they left, I edged nearer to him, 'My dear palmist, you beat me again. How the hell did you know everything about that guy?'

'Ha, simple yaar, the girl is my daughter - my best weapon,' he winked at me for the second time.

The Date

"Why on earth," said JK, "would any sane person do something like that?"

"It's love. It makes you do anything, like what I am doing with you right now," I touched her knees with mine. She smiled and looked down at her plate.

I sipped my coffee and looked at her over the brim. She picked up a piece of mutton with her fork. She stopped halfway.

We were in a suburban restaurant having dinner.

"It's freaky to me.... to meet someone totally stranger and that too someone who you met over Facebook."

"But she's like that."

"Why do you always have to support her craziness?"

"See, if she wants a little adventure, what's the harm in that?"

"But, hey, easy," she looked at me and swallowed some water before saying, "but there are zillions of other ways to meet guys!

What if something bad happens? I would blame you. You should have stopped her."

"Oh, c'mon, it's been a while now since we broke up," I brought my left hand up on the table, "and she's trying hard to move on. I want her to be happy, you know that, I should support her if she wants to meet people to get me out of her system instead of going into depression."

"But she's becoming virtual. It's not how you meet people. How can you know somebody from their profile? How will you know it's not fake?"

"What fake?"

"Everything!"

"You are just panicking. As it is, you come to know about it. She has been chatting with the guy for some time now. I think she knows what she is doing. And it's not that..."

"It's impossible to tell the difference until and unless you stay, or-or at least meet with the person two-three times. You can't know a person over the net, why don't you understand?"

"Hey, why are you so hot about it? It's not my problem if she wants to meet some stranger. Don't speak to me in that tone of yours. Why don't you just go over to her and tell her yourself? And it's not that she is alone. We are also here, no?"

We both looked at the table by the window. My ex-girlfriend seemed to be listening to her date with interest.

"Look, how interesting they seem to be into each other. Do you think that guy is a serial killer? Look, she is interested in him, I tell you. See the way she is keeping her fingers on the table. They are firm. She always does that when something interests her, and see the way she is...."

"Are you sure you have moved on? Look at you, oh my God, you still love her."

Love

'Sufiyana! Sufiyana!' father called out loud as he entered the gate so that my sister, who was sleeping upstairs, could hear him. He was just returning from his morning walk. It was a chilly winter morning. Everybody was under thick quilts; none dared to show their face to the bites of so shivering a cold. And my sister was no exception. 'Sufiyana! Sufiyana!', he continued as there was no answer. My sister found it hard to ignore the loud voice. She woke up. Reluctantly, with sleepy eyes and shivering, she went downstairs and was about to ask what it was when she suddenly caught with her half-opened eyes, a black puppy with some white patches here and there! She forgot all about her sleep and cold! So cute the little creature was that was couching near father's *meiphu!*

'He has been following me from *Khetri,*' father said, caressing the animal tenderly. 'I will get some milk for him,' said my sister and went towards the kitchen. She returned with a bowl of milk and placed it near the confused creature. He licked the plate clean in a matter of a few seconds.

*****

'Pitroo, you're quite dirty! Come, you must have a bath,' commanded my sister to her seven-month-old buddy, who was playing nearby. He wagged his tail vigorously as she lifted him in her arms and carried him into the bathroom. Little Pitroo jumped when he felt the water. 'It's over, it's over,' sister cajoled him repeatedly, as she scrubbed him.' Wow! Our Pitroo looks so handsome!' She let him dry in the sun for a while before she freed him.' Go now, you can play.'

It was a known fact in our *leikai* that the bonding between Sufiyana and her Pitroo was like that of opposite poles of two magnets. It was an unconditional bond. Since that day when her father had brought him, she had become attached to him, or was it he to her? Nobody knew, who cared? They forgot everything else when they saw the pair. She cared for him as if he were more than a pet. He would follow her wherever she went. He would obey her and would do whatever she told him to do. And in return, he would get big hugs and lots of biscuits. Sometimes we teased him, and needless to say, we got spanks from her for doing so.

*****

Pitroo was three years old now. He became mature; he knew how to bite. He began to hunt down birds. He would bark, and children would run away from him, frightened. And he would bark at them again, thinking they were playing! It became a problem - the fact that he began to hunt down hens, ducks and birds in our *leikai*. He would roam in search of lone prey. Sometimes, we would find a chicken head or a dead duckling or a bird's feathers on the floor. It made us sick. My sister would beat him whenever such things happened, but then how stern would a mother's chastise be to her child! So, he would not stop, like a pampered child. He became a nuisance. It was true there were also other dogs in our *leikai* but only two of them lived in the immediate neighbourhood.

And it was also true that Pitroo did the job more often than the other. People who used to admire his beauty and cleverness now began to disgust him, or rather fear him. Complaints began to pour in. My father would pacify them, and they would forget only to come back again. But Pitroo didn't stop his wild act. At times, compensation had to be paid for the losses he had caused. At last, though against my sister's wishes, he was chained. But it was for a short time; when things calmed down, he was freed again. We thought he would stop his bad habits. We were wrong. More complaints arrived. My sister and father did not have a clue what to do.

People began to beat him, shoo him whenever they saw him. They threw stones at him. People who once loved him were now ready to kill him. Whenever a complaint made itself into our house, my brothers and mother would insist sister give him up. She would not listen. And there was her father for her support.

*****

It was a warm autumn morning. My father had just had his meal and was about to take a nap when he saw, through his window, many youths rushing in through our gate. They had sticks, long evil evil-looking sticks in their hands. Father knew what it was all about.

'*Chacha*, today also your dog killed two of Hyderali's ducklings,' they said with a mixture of anger and respect.

'*Mamma*, think yourself too how many times he has killed and eaten our hens and ducks. You don't keep him in chains also. We can't keep our poultry only,' said a tall youth from behind without pretending his anger.

Father heard them patiently. Today, the youths refused to go back without a promise, not to let the dog free again. He could feel the heat but didn't show as he said,' I won't let him loose from today. Pardon him for this last time.'

'That's what you said last time also,' shouted the same tall youth.

'I assure you it won't happen again,' father said confidently. He was a man who was not accustomed to being bullied, that's too by these young punks. But he had to be cool. They were right. They had the right to be angry. It was for the love of Pitroo that he remained calm.

'This is the last time we will show him any pity,' they chorused at the end. Then they dispersed, murmuring amongst themselves. Father looked worried. He returned to his room in heavy steps.

From the veranda upstairs, my sister saw everything. She relieved her hand that was suppressing the poor Pitroo's muzzle from barking. When at last, they were all gone, she let him go. He ran down fast into his master's room. But it was a very hostile place that he had arrived into, at least as of now. So he retreated and sat outside.

'Why don't you understand? 'said my mother,' Sell him off and buy another which is more docile if you can't live without dogs. We are tired of hearing these thugs coming here as if we have done a great crime.'

'Why don't we just sell him away?' It was from my eldest brother.

'Ash! Go away, you all!' Father shooed them away. One by one, they went out. As if on cue, Pitroo came in.

'Pitroo,' it was a voice of love and dejection that came out of my father's lips. The dog silently sat down near the foot of the bed, as if he too knew what it was all about.

Father paced up and down the room before sitting down to think. He thought and thought. After a few uneasy minutes, he called out for his sister. She was weeping without any sound upstairs. She came down after making sure her tears were properly dried off.

'It will be real trouble if we keep him any longer. Our love can't control his behaviour, what can we do?' my father was saying. She was listening.

'There's no alternative. Let's sell him off and buy another one later. Don't worry, we will buy another soon.'

She was a little surprised by the resolution being taken. *What made him take such a decision? Doesn't he know they will slaughter him?* Her mind was in total confusion. Father was looking at her for an answer.

'Yes, father,' she replied slowly. Father saw her disappointment but said nothing.

She went to her room and poured down the tears that were rising from her rickety heart.

Father rode away on his scooter. He returned after half an hour. It was beginning to get dark.

*****

There were three men around him. Father was among them. Ropes were in his hands. One of the two men held a gunny bag. Father squatted near the muzzle of his beloved Pitroo. He slowly began to tie the rope around it.

'Bow-ou-ou,' the dog woke up from his sleep at the feel of a human touch.

'Pitroo! Pitroo!' soothed his master. As it was his master, he didn't bother. Maybe it was his injection day today. Whenever there was a vaccination to be done, it was like that only.

Even when his father tied up his limbs, he didn't make a protest. The faith could be seen. But then, when they tried to put him inside the bag, his suspicion grew.

'Oo-ou-oo,' he cried for help, struggling to free himself. Sister suppressed her anguish and despair as she looked at her poor Pitroo being subjected to such cruelty. *His master doesn't hear his cry for mercy.* Father was busy putting him inside the gunny bag, which the young man was holding. The bag was tied. All's done. The taller of the two gave

Rs.300 to my father. He refused it. The man insisted. Father still refused. Seeing the futility to insist the man pocketed the money. They went away on their moped with the gunny bag on the lap of the pillion rider.

She ran up to the gate and saw her Pitroo struggling inside the bag as they vanished down the dark road. As the sound of the moped died into silence, a single drop of tears ran down near my sister's nose. She tried to hide it from her father with her *chuni*. But he already knew.